FAIRY School

The Best
Book Ever!

by Gail Herman
illustrated by Fran Gianfriddo

WITHDRAWN

A Skylark Book
New York · Toronto · London · Sydney · Auckland

RL 2.5, 006–009

THE BEST BOOK EVER!

A Bantam Skylark Book / November 1999

ISBN 0-553-48682-9

Published simultaneously in the United States and Canada

PRINTED IN THE UNITED STATES OF AMERICA

CWO   0   9   8   7   6   5   4   3   2   1

For my sisters, Randi and Robin

Chapter 1

B-r-r-i-i-n-g! The school bell chimed. Trina Larkspur, a tiny fairy three inchworms high, jumped in surprise. The day was over already? She slipped her lily-pad notebook and feather pen into her fairypack and sighed. She'd been writing a new recipe for early-morning frost and hated to stop. But she'd just have to freeze those ice crystals tomorrow.

Trina loved creating special recipes for frost and dewdrops, and fog and mist. In fact, Trina loved everything about Fairy School. She loved her teacher, Ms. Periwinkle. She loved the leafy green school-tree and the squeaky barkboard at the front of the class branch. She loved having her friends—Belinda Dentalette, Olivia Skye, and Dorrie Windmist—in the same class. Most of all, she loved learning everything there was to know about being a fairy—and mastering each and every skill.

"Before you go, I'd like to assign some homework," Ms. Periwinkle called to the students as they prepared to fly off. "In two days, everyone must hand in a book report. You may report on any book you like."

Book reports! Trina grinned. That was something to be excited about. Every time book reports were handed in, the spider librarian picked a special one to hang in the library for all the fairy students to read. And Trina's book reports had been chosen more often than any other fairy's. She'd love to write about a book she hadn't read yet, one filled with all sorts of amazing adventures. If she could find one.

Just then Belinda flitted next to her. "What book do you think you'll write about?" Belinda's wings moved so fast as she hovered in the air that her whole body vibrated and her fairy sneaker laces came undone.

"I don't know yet." Trina peered at her friend seriously through her straight dark bangs. "But I want it to be extra-special. I mean, really wonderful. Maybe even the best book ever!"

"The best book ever?" Olivia repeated softly, fluttering closer.

"Yes," said Trina. "I'm going to the school library right now."

"Let's all go!" Dorrie called from her toadstool-desk. "We can choose books together!"

"Okay!" Belinda noticed her laces and suddenly stopped jumping. "I just have to tie my shoes."

Olivia turned back to her desk and slipped leaf covers over her prized paintbrushes. "And I just have to put my supplies away."

"Let me help you," Dorrie offered. She whirled around to face Olivia, knocking feather pens and pencils to the ground. "Oops," she said with a laugh, swooping down to pick everything up. "That's not much help."

"Going to the library?" A fairy student named Laurel flew next to Trina and sneered. "You mean little Ms. Smartywings, the smartest fairy in school, doesn't have a book picked out yet?"

Trina shook her head. Laurel could be so mean. She didn't bother to answer.

"Well, I knew which book I'd pick as soon as Ms. Periwinkle announced the assignment. Actually, I started to write my report weeks ago—as soon as I finished the last one!" Laurel said. "And this time, *my* report is going to be hanging in the library. Not yours!"

Laurel flapped her wings furiously and took off, leaving the other fairies staring after her.

"She's so jealous!" Belinda said.

Trina shrugged. "I'm not going to worry about Laurel now. I'm too excited about finding a book. Let's go!"

Chapter 2

A few minutes later, the four friends landed on the library branch.

"Well, hello, fairies," the spider librarian called as they fluttered over. He waved a book in each of his eight arms. Then he shelved them all neatly in a walnut bookcase.

"Guess what, Mr. Spider?" Trina said. "We have another book report to do!"

She gazed at the rows and rows of books.

She'd read each and every one—twice. None of them were special enough for this report. "Do you have any—"

"New books?" Mr. Spider finished for her.

"I guess I've been asking that question a lot lately." Trina blushed. Sometimes she got bored with the same old fairy tales. "But do you?"

Mr. Spider patted her gently with four arms. "I'm sorry, Trina. Not today."

"That's all right," Trina said. But her wings wilted in disappointment.

Mr. Spider gazed at her for a long moment. Then he nodded. "Wait here. I may be able to help you after all."

He scuttled away just as Dorrie shouted from across the branch, "Hey, Trina!" She clapped a wing over her mouth. "Oops! Too loud! Can you help me find a book?" she added in a whisper. "There are so many to choose from!"

Trina looked at Dorrie seriously. Should she recommend a book about cleaning up clutter, since Dorrie was always dropping things and leaving rooms in a mess? Hmmm. Dorrie had just met her fairy godmother. . . .

"How about the fairy godmother story? The one where a fairy godmother helps that Big Person named Cinderella?"

"Great!" said Dorrie.

Trina knew the library so well, she flew to the right shelf, took the second book from the left without even looking at the cover, and handed it to her friend.

"How about me?" asked Olivia.

Trina flew to the art section. Olivia was a talented artist. She shaped the softest, fluffiest clouds and carved the prettiest snowflakes. "Here's one of my favorite books—a collection of autumn leaves, with suggestions for mixing fall colors."

"Perfect!" exclaimed Olivia.

Next Trina helped Belinda choose a book on fairy gymnastics, filled with pictures of tall, grown-up fairies tumbling from cloud to cloud, flipping off stars, and sliding down the Rainbow Bridge to Earth-Below.

"Trina!" Mr. Spider called from the back of the branch, hidden by leaves. "I've found something I think you'll like. Come here, please!"

Trina flew past dense twigs and leaves to a room she'd never known was there. Inside, Mr. Spider was blowing dust off the biggest book she'd ever seen.

"I've been saving this book for a long time," Mr. Spider said softly. "*My* librarian gave it to me after I'd read every book in the

spider school library. I've been waiting to give it to someone who loves books as much as I do."

"Wh-Wh-What kind of book is it?" Trina stammered.

"Why, it's the best book ever! And it's for you!"

Chapter 3

Trina gasped. The best book ever! And it was hers to keep!

She stared at the cover: It showed a Little Big Person Trina guessed must be in first grade too, sitting on a grassy hill while teeny-tiny fairies fluttered all around. Underneath the words *The Best Book Ever* was another title: *Suzy's Adventures in Fairyland.*

It would be perfect for the book report, Trina realized.

"This is a Little Big Person's book," Mr. Spider explained. "And it's about a Little Big Person. But our best happily-ever-after fairies sprinkled it with special fairy dust. So now a new adventure appears every morning. You can read this book forever."

"A new adventure every day! It's a book that never ends!" Trina smiled. "Can I show my friends?"

"Sure. After all, this book is so big, you'll need help bringing it home!"

✳✳✳

Trina called Belinda, Olivia, and Dorrie into the back room. The fairy friends flitted slowly around the giant book, amazed at its size.

Olivia flew up close to the picture of the

Little Big Girl on the cover. "She looks nice," she told Trina.

Suzy had short red curls and a big grin that was missing two teeth.

"She does look nice," Trina agreed. "I can't wait to get this book to my tree-house and start reading."

"How should we carry it?" Belinda asked. "It's so heavy, I'm not sure we can fly with it."

"Well, let's try," Dorrie said. She scooted to the top and grabbed a corner. The other fairies took one corner each.

"Ready, set, fly!" said Trina. The fairies flapped their wings, straining with the effort. The book didn't budge.

"Here," said the spider librarian. "Allow me to call some friends." Mr. Spider whistled, and a swarm of bees hurried over.

"Need some help?" the Queen Bee asked. "My workers aren't buzzzzzy at all."

"Yes, please!" said Trina.

The bees whizzed through the air, with the fairies following as quickly as they could. Trina swept past Laurel. The mean fairy was standing by the Babbling Brook, ordering some turtles to form a bridge so she could step across the water without getting her toes wet.

"You there!" she bossed one small turtle. "Get in line."

"Why don't you just fly across?" the little turtle protested.

"If I wanted to fly, I would. But I want to walk, so . . ." Laurel looked up and spied the big book flying through the air. Trina could see Laurel's look of surprise as she watched the four fairy friends way up in the sky.

Then, in no time at all, the giant book was standing in Trina's backyard.

Belinda settled on the grass and licked one of the honey-sticks the bees had passed around. "Okay, that's done. Now, who wants to go to Fairyland Meadow and slide down the waterfall?"

"Me!" cried Dorrie.

"Me too," Olivia said. She smiled at Trina. "Are you coming? Or do you want to stay home and read the book?"

"I'm going to stay right here," Trina declared. "Thanks for helping me get it home."

"You're welcome!" the friends chorused as they flew away. "Make sure to tell us about Suzy!" Olivia called back.

"Okay!"

Trina fluttered close to the book, then landed on the cover. She grasped one end and flew in a half-circle, opening it to the first page. "There!"

She was just about to start reading when her parents flew into the backyard.

"Is this giant book yours?" Mrs. Larkspur's voice rose with astonishment.

"Wherever did it come from?" asked Mr. Larkspur.

Trina explained about the book report, Mr. Spider, and his surprise gift.

Mr. and Mrs. Larkspur smiled at their daughter. "That's wonderful! Let's see if we have room for it inside the tree trunk, or on a branch."

Trina followed her parents into their tree-house. Sighing, Mrs. Larkspur waved a wing at the already cluttered tree, filled with fairy-sized books, papers, and pinecone paperweights.

"One of these days, we'll have to stop

bringing work home with us," Mr. Larkspur said, shaking his head.

Trina's parents worked in the Fairyland Museum, and their home was filled with all sorts of items waiting to be used in exhibits.

Trina opened the ice-block refrigerator to take a glass of nectar. A snowflake carved by the artist Magdalena—all set for the museum's Winter Wonderland Weekend—sat inside.

"Oh, please keep bringing things home," Trina said. "I love to see what's going on at the museum. I'll just keep the book outside, right where it is."

✳✳✳

A few minutes later, Trina settled on the backyard grass, ready to begin *The Best Book Ever*.

Suzy believed in fairies, she read. Then she

couldn't read any more for a few minutes. She was laughing too hard.

"What a funny way to start a book! Why wouldn't Suzy believe in fairies?"

And every night Suzy dreamed about fairies, Trina continued reading. *She dreamed she could fly with them through starry nights and use their magic to talk to birds and bees and flowers and trees. She wanted to know where fairies lived. She wanted to play their games. "There are no such things as fairies," Suzy's mother told her. But Suzy knew better. There were fairies out there. And Suzy planned to find them.*

Trina read on and on, all about Suzy's adventures with fairies. She was such a fast reader, she had read the entire book by bedtime and even started her book report.

But what about tomorrow? she thought. There's a brand-new adventure coming in the morning. One I haven't read yet. And I should use that in the book report too!

So as soon as the sun peeked through her knothole window the next morning, Trina flew outside to open her book.

" 'Suzy and the Sparrow,' " she read the chapter title excitedly. Then she went on to read the story.

"Trina!" called her mom. "Come inside and eat breakfast, or you'll be late for school."

"Oh!" Trina said. She'd been planning on adding the story to her report right away. "I'll have to work on it later."

And then she realized something else: If there was a new story every day, how would she ever finish her book report?

Chapter 4

That morning, just as usual, Trina met her friends by the weeping willow tree to fly to school together. At their class branch, they stood by their toadstool-desks and recited the Fairy School Pledge. Then they had tooth fairy class, followed by a rainbow-sliding lesson and wish-granting.

It was a day like any other. But Trina kept glancing at a cuckoo-clock bird flying past.

Trina tapped her wings and waited impatiently for the morning to end. She could barely pay attention to Ms. Periwinkle. She kept thinking about *The Best Book Ever* and the book report. She just had to get back to work! If she finished writing about "Suzy and the Sparrow" that afternoon, she could read the new story in the morning and work on it the *next* afternoon.

She stole a look at the cuckoo-clock bird again. Only 11:30.

Why oh why was this day taking so long?

Suddenly she realized Ms. Periwinkle was making an announcement.

". . . then the school will be open as usual."

"What's going on?" Trina whispered to Dorrie.

"The school tree is going to be pruned

in a few minutes," Dorrie told her. "We all have to leave." Dorrie giggled. "Get it? Leave?"

"You'll have some free time, outside of school," Ms. Periwinkle continued. "I think you should use it to work on your book reports."

"I don't need any extra time," Laurel bragged. "My book report is already the best I've ever written." She looked at Trina and turned up her nose. "Probably the best anyone's ever written!"

"I just want *everyone* to do their best," Ms. Periwinkle went on patiently.

A group of june bugs peeked in through the leaves. "We're ready to start pruning," one announced, already nibbling a leaf.

Just then the school bell chimed and Ms. Periwinkle clapped her wings. "All right, class. You have about two hours. Please come back to school when you hear the bell chime again. Now, have a good study time!"

Belinda flapped around excitedly, gathering her things. "This study time is great! We can do our work in Fairyland Meadow, under the weeping willow tree!"

Olivia came over to them, tucking her hair behind her ears. "We can go right now, if everyone has their book."

"I do!" Dorrie pulled *Cinderella* from under a pile of books, and everything clattered noisily to the branch.

"What about you, Trina?" Olivia asked. Then, before Trina could answer, she said, "I forgot! Of course, *The Best Book Ever* is at your house. We can all help you carry it, if you like."

"No, thanks," Trina said. She wanted to

spend every single second working—not fig-uring out a way to move the book. "I'll just meet you back at school."

Trina rushed home from school, eager to begin. These extra two hours were exactly what she needed. Now, what should she say about "Suzy and the Sparrow"?

For a long moment, she sat cross-legged in her backyard, just staring at the giant book propped up against her tree-house. She grinned at the picture of Suzy on the cover. Suzy grinned back.

"If only Suzy could talk," Trina said, without really thinking. "Then she could tell me about her adventures, the ones I've read and the ones I haven't. And then I could finish my report."

Trina clapped her wings. That was it! She'd bring Suzy out of the book. They could discuss so many things! She'd really know Suzy and would be able to write about her for the book report.

But how could she make Suzy come to life? By reciting a spell? By tossing fairy dust?

Maybe the best thing would be to use a spell *and* fairy dust—double fairy power for such a hard job.

Trina pulled her fairy-dust bag out of her fairypack, along with her magic wand. Then she waved her wand once, twice, three times, tapped the book, and said: *"Suzy, Suzy, Little Big Girl. Come and play when you see dust whirl. Now I see you in the book. But out you'll be, when next I look."*

Taking a deep breath, Trina flicked a handful of fairy dust. It swooped around the book . . . once, twice, three times. The book began to spin. Faster and faster it whirled, until its pages were only a blur. Then it rose in the air, high above the tree-house.

"Oh, no!" Trina groaned. "What have I done? The book is going to fly away!"

She flew after the book, hoping to catch it or stop it or something. But the book floated back down to the backyard and settled on the grass—lying open.

Is that it? Trina wondered. Is the magic over?

Not exactly.

The book began to quiver and tremble and shake and quake.

Suddenly Suzy tumbled out.

"Oh!" Trina was so surprised, she hung in midair. Suzy was sooo big. Her foot was the size of a fairy football field. Her hand was as tall as a fairy-sized Christmas tree.

Suzy somersaulted from the book to the soft grass—heading straight for the treehouse. *Bang!* Her feet bumped hard against the trunk. The tree shook with the jolt. *Crash!* Trina heard shell-dishes clatter to the floor. *Boom!* That must be the cups, Trina thought.

Everything quieted down, and Trina flew close to Suzy. The Little Big Person lay on the ground, gazing around in confusion. Finally she looked at the tiny fairy, no bigger than her finger.

"Are you okay?" Trina asked, hovering by Suzy's face. "Come! Sit and lean against the tree. That was some bump!"

"I feel fine," Suzy said slowly as she rested against the trunk. She swung her head around to peer into Trina's bedroom window—a knothole way up on the third floor.

"Oh, what a cute room!" she exclaimed. "It's like a little dollhouse! But where am I?" She turned to squint again at Trina. "And who are you?"

"I'm a fairy named Trina. And I called you out of the book so we could talk."

"Really, truly?" Suzy beamed. "You mean this isn't another story? I'm for real now?" She pointed at the book. "Hey! I'm not on the cover anymore! I'm all here! Trina, you must be a real, honest-to-goodness fairy."

Trina nodded and explained the magic of Fairyland. She was just telling Suzy about her book report, when she heard Olivia, Dorrie, and Belinda calling from the front of her tree.

"Those are my friends," Trina whispered to Suzy. "I'd better tell them about you before they actually see you."

"You mean I'll get to see even more fairies?" Suzy asked.

"Trina! Who are you talking to? We thought you'd be alone, but . . ." Belinda suddenly raced around the tree trunk talking, but trailed off as she spied Suzy.

Dorrie and Olivia flew behind her, and all three fairies skidded to a stop. Olivia rubbed her eyes. "Suzy?" she asked.

Trina giggled. "Yes, it's Suzy!"

"Sh-She's so . . . b-big!" Belinda stammered.

"Of course," Trina answered. "She's a Little Big Person! I made her real to help me with my book report."

"She doesn't look so little to me," Dorrie said in a whisper. "A *big* Big Person must be humongous!"

"So what are you going to do with her?" Olivia asked Trina.

"I'm going to talk to her." Trina smiled at Suzy. "Can you tell me more about your adventures?"

Suzy told Trina about the fairies she met in the book and her friends and family. Then she explained what it was like to be a Little Big Person who loved fairies, and her dream of making fairy magic all by herself.

Trina wrote down everything, jotting notes and saying, "Aha!"

"That's it!" Suzy said finally.

"That's wonderful," said Trina. "Thanks for your help. Now I'll be able to write a really great book report."

"Now it's your turn to help me!" Suzy leaped to her feet. The thud echoed through the yard, and the fairies jumped back in surprise. "You read in my book how I want to be like a fairy?"

Trina nodded.

"Well, that's what I want to do right now! I want to play tag with butterflies, and I want to hop from lily pad to lily pad with little frogs."

"You can't!" Olivia said worriedly. "You're too big."

Suzy went on as if she hadn't heard. "And do you know what I want to do most of all?"

"What?" asked Trina.

"Something magical."

"But you don't know the first thing about being a fairy," Dorrie added. "Believe me, it's not as easy as it looks."

Suzy shrugged. "You'll help me, won't you, Trina?"

Before Trina could answer, Suzy spied an ant family having a picnic in the far corner of Trina's yard. "Look!" she said. "They can be my new friends too! In Fairyland ants can talk. But they don't in my book."

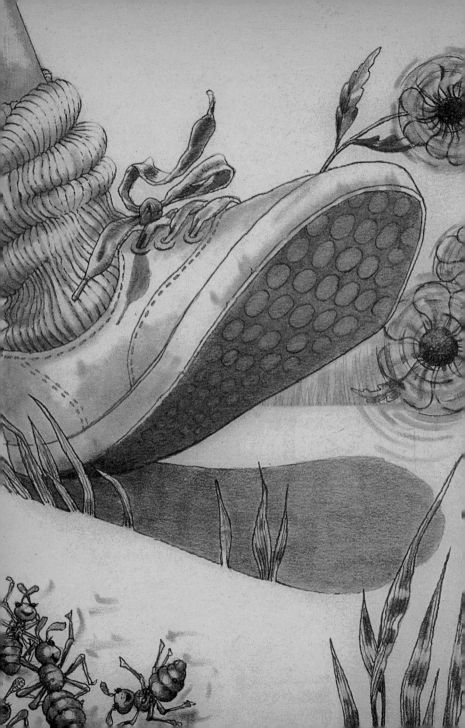

In a flash, she leaped into the air.

"Oh, no!" Olivia gasped. "She's going to land right on them!"

"Daisies!" Trina called quickly to some nearby flowers. "I need a windstorm. Now!"

Immediately the daisies spun their petals like fans. The wind blew so hard and fast, the ants were sent flying to safety . . . just as Suzy landed on their spot.

Suzy scrambled around, trying to find the ants, and the fairies flew to join her.

"You brought a Big Person out of a book—and didn't ask permission from your parents or Ms. Periwinkle!" Olivia whispered to Trina. "This is going to be *big* trouble!"

"That's right," Belinda said. "She almost squished those poor ants. She's so big, who knows what else she might do?"

Dorrie watched Suzy accidentally squash

a fairy-berry patch with the heel of her sneaker. "You'd better put her back in her book," Dorrie added, "before she does anything worse than smash berries!"

"What are you talking about?" said Suzy. She forgot her search for the ants and knelt to talk to the fairies as they perched on a tree root. "You want me to go back inside my book? Already?"

"Wel-l-l . . . ," Trina said.

"I'm sorry about the berries," Suzy said quickly. "But you can't send me back so quickly. Please, Trina. I want to be just like a fairy. Just for a little while." She squatted down gingerly and tried to repair the berries. "I'll be more careful! I promise!"

Trina gazed at Suzy, amazed she was there at all. The whole thing was too exciting to be believed. A real live Big Person in Fairyland! And Suzy had really helped her with the book report. She had to do something nice for Suzy too.

"Suzy can stay," Trina announced. "But only for a little while. Until we go back to school."

There's not much time before the school bell chimes, she thought. What could possibly happen?

Chapter 5

"I can stay! I can stay!" Suzy clapped her hands happily. "What should we do first?" she asked. "Take a sun shower? Slide down a waterfall slide?"

Dorrie laughed. "You're so tall, you'd think the waterfall was just a little drip."

"I think we should stay right here," Trina cautioned. There was no telling what might happen with a Big Person trooping around Fairyland.

Suzy shook her head, and her red curls bounced. "That's no fun, Trina. I really, really, really want to see Fairyland."

Trina nodded reluctantly. Bringing Suzy out of the book had been all her idea. And it wouldn't be fair if Suzy didn't at least get a peek around Fairyland.

"All right," she agreed. "But we'll only go to Fairyland Meadow."

"Is that where you play?" Suzy asked. "Once I see where you play, I'll go right back home. I promise."

She hopped up and down, then jumped up on the bottom branch of the tree-house. "Which way do we go? Can I see it from here?" She climbed to the next branch, and the one after that, breaking off little twigs as she went.

"Ouch! Ouch!" cried the tree-house.

"Oops!" Suzy stopped and patted the tree. "Everything here is like a person. How amazing! I'm sorry, tree."

The tree bowed.

Just then, while Suzy was hidden by the branches and leaves, Trina heard a familiar voice.

"Oh, Trina! My good friend Trina. Where are you?"

"It's Laurel!" Trina whispered. "Belinda, tell Suzy to keep quiet! I don't want Laurel to find out she's here."

Belinda darted up into the branches as Laurel flew closer to Trina. "I was just checking to see how your book report is coming along, Trina. I'm finished with mine," Laurel said smugly. "*All* my book reports. With the extra time, I just did another one. I'm sure I'll get credit for handing in two! And I bet Mr. Spider will be only too happy to hang up both in the library."

"That's nice, Laurel." Trina gazed anxiously at the leaves. Could Laurel see anything strange up there?

"So what have you been working on?" Laurel asked.

"Oh, nothing too exciting. Would you excuse me, please? I'm right in the middle."

Laurel grinned. "You mean you haven't finished? Well, maybe I'll just stick around, in case you need any help."

Trina knew Laurel didn't want to help. She only wanted to spy.

"No, thanks."

Trina waited for Laurel to leave. But Laurel didn't seem to be going anywhere.

Humming a little tune, Laurel wandered over to *The Best Book Ever*.

Uh-oh, Trina thought. There's no Suzy in

the book! She crossed her wings for luck. Maybe Laurel wouldn't notice.

Laurel looked at the book curiously. "This seems odd," she said. "What—"

"Yoo-hoo, Laurel!" Belinda suddenly circled overhead. "I just wrote a second book report too!"

"You did? What is it on? Oh, never mind, I'll just do a third. Maybe on the Bumblebee Ball, or Tinkerbell . . . or . . . something!" Laurel darted away without another glance at Trina.

Belinda grinned. "That should take care of her for a while."

But Trina didn't feel so sure.

Chapter 6

Okay, Trina thought. Suzy can stay long
enough to see Fairyland Meadow. But we
just can't have her racing around looking like
a Big Person, she realized. We'll all get in
trouble for letting Suzy into Fairyland. She
needs a disguise!

Minutes later, Trina and her friends had
dressed Suzy with twigs and leaves, stuck on
with fairy dust. "There!" said Trina. "If any

fairy comes along, stay very still. If they don't look too closely, they'll think you're a tree."

The fairies only had one hour left before they had to be back in school. So Trina and her friends set off quickly. They had to slow down right away, though. Even though Suzy had long legs, she was wrapped so tightly with fairy branches that she could only take baby steps.

Even worse, the little twigs in Suzy's costume tickled her nose, making her stop and sneeze over and over again. Leaves blew off with every *achoo!* and dropped on passing birds and bugs.

"Sorry," Dorrie kept apologizing to the creatures. "This tree has hay fever!"

"Now, remember," Trina said to Suzy. "You're wearing a disguise, but if any tall fairies find us, they'll see through your disguise for sure if you sneeze. So stay out of sight."

Then Trina giggled. Suzy was so big, it seemed impossible for her to be out of sight. "At least try to be invisible," she added.

"Maybe if I wish to be invisible with all my heart, then no one will see me," Suzy said. "Wouldn't that be like fairy magic?"

"It sure would," Trina agreed.

"Well, let's get moving," Suzy said seriously. "And I'll start wishing." She pushed the twigs away from her face, then waddled along the ground, hiding behind trees and ducking behind big plants.

Trina and her friends flew next to Suzy, and Trina took a deep breath.

Maybe this will work after all, she thought. Suzy *is* being very quiet. And while they were getting some strange looks from the birds and bugs, Trina didn't know any of them by name. Maybe, just maybe, no other fairy would find out.

Then she peered back and saw the grass behind them, trampled down by Suzy's feet. It looked like a giant path. A new road—for Big People!

"Come on," Trina said to her friends. "Help me fix the grass so it's straight before any fairies see it! Suzy, hide for a second."

The fairies flew back, trying to pull up each blade of grass.

"Thank you," one blade said. "That position is terrible for my back!"

Trina sighed. There was so much grass still bent in half! They really weren't making much of a difference.

Wait a minute! Did she hear wings fluttering? She glanced up and thought she saw

Laurel's colorful wings flapping behind a cloud. She was just about to fly up and investigate when Suzy called loudly.

"Hey, everybody!" she shouted from her hiding place behind a big boulder. "What are you doing?"

Trina stopped. Suzy's voice was so strong, it sent a giant gust of wind blowing toward the fairies.

"Help, help!" cried a tiny ladybug, caught in the current. "I can't stop!"

Belinda dove into the draft, hugged the ladybug against her chest, and flew back out, battling the wind.

"Are you okay?" Trina asked the little bug.

"I guess so." The ladybug straightened her bent antenna. "What was that—a storm?"

"Something like that," Trina told her. She

looked up at the clouds. No Laurel anywhere. Maybe she'd imagined it. Shrugging, she darted over to Suzy. "No more trampling on grass," she lectured. "And no more shouting. You almost blew a ladybug all the way to the Rainbow Bridge."

"The Rainbow Bridge!" Suzy exclaimed. "Can we go there too?"

Trina and her friends answered all together with a loud *"NO!"*

If we *really* hurry, Trina thought, we can see Fairyland Meadow, then have Suzy back in the book in no time. But Suzy was stopping at practically every tree, wanting to see the sights.

"Oh, look! Apples!" Suzy exclaimed when they passed a small grove. "I'm starving!"

"Do you mind?" she asked an apple tree. The tree was so surprised to see a Big Person, it couldn't even speak. "I guess that means you don't mind," said Suzy. She picked some apples, ate quickly, and tossed the cores on the ground. Then she grabbed some oranges and dropped the peels as she ate. Suzy was so excited! She raced around like a whirlwind, sending a group of beehives spinning.

Trina glanced at the sun. Their hour was almost up. There wasn't time to clean the mess. They barely had time to go to Fairyland Meadow!

"We've got to go, Suzy. If you want to see the Meadow, we have to move it *right now!*"

"Yes, ma'am," Suzy yelled. Then she took off running, scattering twigs and branches behind her because she was in such a hurry. Belinda was the only fairy who was fast enough to stay in front of her and give her directions.

Thank goodness Belinda knows how to get

to the Meadow, Trina thought as she huffed and puffed and tried to keep up. If we got lost now it would be bad news.

Finally they all arrived. Good, thought Trina. We can hide Suzy under Mr. Willow for a minute and catch our breaths.

Without thinking, Trina and her friends darted under the branches of the weeping willow tree. Suzy tried to duck under too.

"Waaah!" sobbed Mr. Willow. "A giant is tangled in my leaves! Help! Help!"

"Sorry," Suzy said. "But I can't fit through!"

Maybe hiding under Mr. Willow wouldn't work after all. Trina swooped outside, then hovered high above the crying tree. From there, she could see all of Fairyland—and all the damage Suzy had done. Apple cores and orange peels littered the ground. Insects scrambled out from under them, trying to get free. Grass and twigs were trampled. Giant footprints were sunk in mud puddles. Beehives were spinning. And who knew what else Trina couldn't see! It was much worse than she had thought.

They had to fix Fairyland!

B-r-r-i-i-n-g! School chimes! Trina gasped. It was time to go back to class.

"Trina, I want to see Fairy School too!" Suzy said happily.

Trina groaned. "You have to go back into the book," she said firmly. "Just as you promised." Then she turned to her friends. "I have to clean up, and it will take a while. You'd better get flying so you won't get in trouble for being late back to school."

B-r-r-i-i-n-g!

Belinda shook her head. "We're not going anywhere without you."

"That's right," Olivia added. "We'll help. No matter how long it takes."

"And we'll *all* be late," Dorrie said. "Together."

Trina sighed. It was bad enough for her to be late. She deserved any trouble that came her way, since this whole mess was her fault. Her friends hadn't done anything but try to help. She couldn't let them be late too. It wouldn't be right. But she knew they'd never leave her alone.

"Okay. Here's the plan," she said. "Suzy goes with us to school. We find somewhere for her to hide until I can send her back after class. Then we fix all the messes in Fairyland."

"Hooray!" Suzy clapped her hands.

Trina stared at Suzy. Only a few twigs were left of her leafy green costume. "But,"

Trina continued, "you have to wear your disguise the whole time and hide in the tree next to school. You can peek over. And that's all! No talking, no sneezing, no moving, no nothing!"

Chapter 7

When Trina and her friends flew onto the class branch, Ms. Periwinkle was hovering by the barkboard—as if nothing at all were out of the ordinary. She smiled as the fairy students settled into seats. "How did your book reports go?" she asked.

"Great!" Laurel said loudly. "I wrote a few extra ones, in case you were giving extra credit. I'm sure one of them will be hanging in the library very soon. And I know for a fact that someone"—she shot a look at Trina—"hasn't come close to finishing hers yet! She's been too busy flying around Fairyland."

Trina gulped. Laurel must have been spying all along. And now she was going to tell Ms. Periwinkle that Trina had set a Big Person loose in Fairyland.

Laurel grinned. "And, Ms. Periwinkle, there's something you should know about Trina's book report. She—"

"I'm interested in everyone's book report, Laurel. But let's talk about them later. I'd like to have a falling-star class now, while the sun is still high in the sky and the stars aren't so wide-awake and twinkly."

A falling-star lesson? How could Trina concentrate on that, when all she could think about was Suzy—perched in the crook of a neighboring tree? She looked over at the spot.

If you looked exactly right, you couldn't miss Suzy. Just then, she was waving her arms and stretching and pulling at her legs as if she were stuck.

Oh, no, Trina realized. She *is* stuck!

Trina thought fast. How could she get Suzy unstuck? Belinda was sitting right beside Trina, and Trina whispered to her what had happened.

"We can't do anything now," Belinda said. "Let's wait a few seconds until we fly outside for class."

Good idea, Trina thought. I'll be able to get closer to Suzy then.

"All right, class," Ms. Periwinkle said. "Let's fly up to those stars together."

Laurel rushed past. "Here's something else I can do better than you," she hissed to

Trina. "My star is going to drop faster and brighter than yours!"

Right then, Trina didn't care if Laurel's star was the fastest one in all Fairyland and hers was the slowest. She just wanted Laurel to stop talking so she could think.

While everyone else flew up high, past the clouds, Trina hovered and let them pass.

"Let's get you out of here," she said, flying to Suzy and tugging on an arm.

"Oof!" said Suzy. "You're pulling too hard."

"Here!" Belinda darted over and took the other arm. "Maybe if we both pull at once."

"One, two, three!" counted Trina, and they pulled.

"I'm still stuck!" Suzy moaned.

"Trina? Belinda?" Ms. Periwinkle's voice floated down through leaves and drifting clouds. "Come choose your star."

"We'll be right back," Trina told Suzy, flying away. "And we'll bring Dorrie and Olivia too."

All the fairies were floating next to stars as Trina and Belinda took their places. Trina whispered to her friends, telling them what had happened.

"Now, class," Ms. Periwinkle was saying. "I'll pull some stars closer to the ground for you. But the trick to making a star fall is to persuade that star to move by itself. The happier the star is, the faster it will go."

The first-grade fairies began to talk to their stars, making jokes and silly faces to coax the stars to laugh.

"All right, get cracking," Laurel bossed her glittering star. "I don't have all day. I want you to fall now—hard and fast."

Trina and Belinda flitted close to Dorrie and Olivia. "We'll fly back down to Suzy in

just a minute," Trina whispered, "when no one is looking."

Laurel's star blinked but didn't move an inch. Other stars began to fall, and Laurel turned a bright red.

"Come on!" Laurel shouted. "You're making me look bad!"

Everyone stared at Laurel. "Let's go!" Trina said to her friends.

The four fairies flew back to the tree. They pushed and pulled and prodded Suzy.

"I'm almost out!" Suzy said excitedly. "Just one more tug!"

"Okay!" Trina took a deep breath. "Everybody pull!"

The fairies pulled with all their strength, and Suzy sprang out of the tree. She bounced off her branch and up to the clouds.

"Oops!" said Dorrie. "We should have held on tighter!"

Suzy sailed past cloud after cloud, leaving a trail of leaves behind her. "I'm flying!" she shouted happily. "Just like a real fairy!"

Then she landed right on Laurel's star. The star jumped in surprise. It began to drop.

"Hey, wait a minute!" Laurel said. "You're *my* star!"

Suzy lost her footing. She fell off the star, tumbling and spinning through space. Luckily, Trina and her friends caught her. They fluttered their wings as fast as they could to hold her up in the air.

"Did you see that, Trina?" Suzy said as she hovered in the sky. "I made a falling star! I did fairy magic!"

"You really did!" Trina answered. She felt happy for Suzy—and suddenly realized how much she liked her.

"Look! It's a real live Little Big Person!" a

boy fairy named Sebastian shouted. All the first-graders rushed over to meet Suzy. Only Laurel hung back, her mouth shut tight. Suzy had left her speechless!

Trina giggled. Everything had turned out fine. Better than fine. Perfect, really. Laurel had finally shut her mouth. And Suzy had seen what it was like to be a real fairy. But then Trina heard Ms. Periwinkle call.

"Trina, I think you need to do some explaining here!"

Chapter 8

Trina and Suzy stayed after school to talk to Ms. Periwinkle.

"So Suzy is the character in *The Best Book Ever,* my book for the report." Trina explained how Mr. Spider had given her the book, how she'd brought Suzy out of the book, and how everything had happened after that. At last, out of breath, she finished.

Ms. Periwinkle shook her head. "You

know, Trina, it is very dangerous to let a Little Big Person roam around Fairyland."

"I know, Ms. Periwinkle. But I didn't think it would be so bad. I only wanted Suzy to visit for an hour or so—and only in my backyard. Things just got out of control."

"I'm sorry too," Suzy put in. "I should have listened to Trina when she wanted to put me back. It's just that I wanted to see Fairyland so badly. I didn't mean to make a mess of things."

"All right, girls," Ms. Periwinkle said. "There is only a little harm done. If Suzy lived on Earth-Below, we'd have real trouble. We can't have all those Big People knowing about Fairyland. But since she lives in a book, we'll be just fine."

"So everything's okay?" Trina said hopefully.

"It will be after you fix everything that

Suzy broke. And you apologize to any bugs who were caught under those apples and oranges."

"Of course!" Trina said quickly.

Ms. Periwinkle smiled. "Good. Trina, I'll help you put Suzy back in the book now."

"You know what?" Suzy sighed as they made their way back to Trina's tree. "I'm tired. I'm ready to go home and take a nap."

Trina felt a lump in her throat as she perched in Suzy's palm in front of *The Best Book Ever.* "I'm going to miss you, Suzy. You were fun. You're the only one who could keep Laurel quiet!"

"I'll miss you too, Trina," Suzy said. "But you can see me every time you read my book."

"Now, make up a spell, Trina," Ms. Periwinkle said softly.

Trina raised her wand. *"The time is past for*

you to stay. I'll call again another day. Now hurry back into your book. We'll meet again, next time I look."

Trina fluttered her wings as a whirl of stars spiraled around Suzy, lifting her into the air, then spinning her around and around, between the covers and into the book.

Suzy was gone.

✳✳✳

Trina and her friends spent the rest of the day straightening Fairyland. Then Trina went home and worked on her book report, which was due the next day. Now that she knew so much about Suzy, she didn't worry about new stories she hadn't read yet. She already had lots to say.

The Best Book Ever *is filled with magical tales about a Little Big Person named Suzy,*

Trina wrote. *Even though no one believes her, Suzy knows, deep in her heart, that there are fairies somewhere in the world. And because she is true to her dream, Suzy finds the fairies and has amazing adventures.*

Trina wrote for a long time. When she was finished, she was so tired she fell asleep as soon as her head hit her leaf-pillow.

The next morning, she woke with a start, thinking someone was calling her name.

"Trina!" she heard again. "Come here, please!"

Trina gasped. It sounded like Suzy! But it couldn't be! She darted outside and gazed around. No Suzy anywhere.

"Trina!"

She looked around the yard. Then she saw her book. The picture of Suzy on the cover seemed to wink.

Trina shook her head. Was she seeing

things? She flipped some pages to the back and saw a new story: "Suzy Goes to Fairy-land."

"It's my story!" Trina said, reading through it quickly. "It tells all about my spell and everything that happened."

Suzy winked again, and Trina smiled at her new friend. "This really *is* the best book ever!" Trina said.

The Fairy School Pledge

(sung to the tune of "Twinkle, Twinkle, Little Star")

We are fairies
Brave and bright.
Shine by day,
Twinkle by night.

We're friends of birds
And kind to bees.
We love flowers
And the trees.

We are fairies
Brave and bright.
Shine by day,
Twinkle by night.